Library
Volunteers
Are in the
Spotlight

In honor of volunteer

Serena Chen

— April 2011 —

Champaign Public
◆》LIBRARY

NANCY DREW

THE NEW CASE FILES

Based on the series by Carolyn Keene Girl Detective®

VAMPIRE SLAYER PART ONE

By Petrucha, Kinney & Murase

PAPERCUTZ™

NANCY DREW GRAPHIC NOVELS AVAILABLE FROM PAPERCUTZ

#1 "The Demon of River Heights"

#2 "Writ In Stone"

#3 "The Haunted Dollhouse"

#4 "The Girl Who Wasn't There"

#5 "The Fake Heir"

#6 "Mr. Cheeters Is Missing"

#7 "The Charmed Bracelet"

#8 "Global Warning"

#9 "Ghost In The Machinery"

#10 "The Disoriented Express"

#11 "Monkey Wrench Blues"

#12 "Dress Reversal"

#13 "Doggone Town"

#14 "Sleight of Dan"

#15 "Tiger Counter"

#16 "What Goes Up..."

#17 "Night of the Living Chatchke"

#18 "City Under the Basement"

#19 "Cliffhanger"

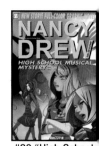

#20 "High School Musical Mystery"

Graphic Novels #1-19 are $7.95 each in paperback, $12.95 hardcover. Graphic Novel #20 is $8.99 in paperback, $13.99 hardcover. Please add $4.00 for postage and handling for the first book, add $1.00 for each additional book. Please make check payable to NBM Publishing. Send to:
Papercutz, 40 Exchange Place, Suite 1308, New York, NY 10005, 1-800-886-1223

www.papercutz.com

NANCY DREW

Based on the series by Carolyn Keene · Girl Detective®

VAMPIRE SLAYER · PART ONE

STEFAN PETRUCHA & SARAH KINNEY • Writers
SHO MURASE • Artist
with 3D CG elements and color by CARLOS JOSE GUZMAN
Based on the series by
CAROLYN KEENE

PAPERCUT Z™
New York

Let me introduce myself. Or did I already? No, probably not—at least not so you'd recognize me. I'm Nancy Drew. My friends call me Nancy. My enemies call me a lot of other things, like "that girl who cooked my goose." They actually sometimes speak like that, but what can you expect from criminals? See, I'm a detective. Not really. I mean, I don't have a license or anything. I don't carry a gun (not that I would touch one of those even if I could) or a badge. I'm not even old enough to have one. But I am old enough to know when something isn't right, when somebody's getting an unfair deal, or when someone's done something they shouldn't do. And I know how to stop them, catch them, and get them into the hands of the law, where they belong. I take those things seriously and I'm almost never wrong.

Not that my best friends Bess and George would agree with that. They tell me I'm wrong a lot, and they have to cover for me all the time just to make me look good. I think that's what best friends do for one another. Bess would tell you I dress badly. I call it casual. George would tell you I'm not focused. By that she'd mean that once again I forgot to fill my car with gas or bring enough money to buy lunch. I'm always focused when it comes to crime. Always.

"Vampire Slayer" Part One
STEFAN PETRUCHA & SARAH KINNEY – Writers
SHO MURASE — Artist
with 3D CG elements and color by CARLOS JOSE GUZMAN
BRYAN SENKA – Letterer
TROY HAHN – Production
MICHAEL PETRANEK – Editorial Assistant
JIM SALICRUP
Editor-in-Chief

ISBN: 978-1-59707-213-7 paperback edition
ISBN: 978-1-59707-214-4 hardcover edition

Printed in China
July 2010 by Asia One Printing LTD.
13/F Asia One Tower
8 Fung Yip St., Chaiwan
Hong Kong

Distributed by Macmillan.

First Printing

THAT'S ME, *NANCY DREW, GIRL DETECTIVE,* THE ONE WITH THE CROSSBOW AND THE ATTITUDE.

I DON'T KNOW *HOW* I LET YOU TWO TALK ME INTO THIS!

COME ON, NANCE! IF WE SHOW UP TO THE MOVIE IN COSTUME WE GET IN FOR HALF PRICE!

AND GEORGE AND I HAVE ALREADY SEEN IT *FOUR* TIMES, SO WE *NEED* TO SAVE SOME MONEY!

THE OTHER TWO ARE MY FRIENDS, GEORGE AND BESS.

USUALLY I'M DRAGGING THEM SOMEPLACE DANGEROUS, SO I FIGURE IT'S ONLY FAIR TO LET THEM DRAG ME OUT ONCE IN A WHILE.

HEY, AT LEAST *YOU* DON'T HAVE FAKE *WEREWOLF* HAIR PLASTERED OVER YOUR FACE!

NOW, NOW! YOU MAKE A *LOVELY* WOLF!

THEN AGAIN, THE SHORTCUT THROUGH THE CEMETERY I SUGGESTED TURNED OUT TO BE MORE DANGEROUS THAN I THOUGHT.

DID YOU GUYS *HEAR* SOME-THING?

AS A DARK FIGURE LEAPT OVER THE GRAVESTONE I WAS THINKING THIS PROBABLY WOULD HAVE BEEN *MUCH* MORE FRIGHTENING IF I ACTUALLY BELIEVED IN VAMPIRES.

THEN I REALIZED, IT WAS PRETTY MUCH AS FRIGHTENING AS IT COULD GET NO MATTER *WHAT* I BELIEVED.

NANCY DREW
VAMPIRE SLAYER PART ONE

NANCY!

WHAT'S THE PLAN?

RUN!

IT WASN'T ALWAYS MY BEST *PLAN*, BUT IT DID WORK SOMETIMES.

UNLESS WHOEVER WAS CHASING YOU TURNS OUT TO BE MUCH *FASTER*.

I'M GENERALLY *NOT* THE VIOLENT TYPE, BUT IT DIDN'T FEEL LIKE I HAD MUCH CHOICE HERE.

OF COURSE THE CROSSBOW WAS *FAKE*, PART OF MY SLAYER COSTUME.

BUT TALL DARK AND *FANGY* HERE DIDN'T KNOW THAT.

AND THAT TRICK **WORKED**.

MOSTLY, I WAS THINKING, "PHEW!"

BUT I WAS ALSO THINKING I'D AT LEAST HAVE A SECOND TO FIGURE OUT WHAT WAS GOING ON.

UNFORTUNATELY, THE FIRST THING I FIGURED OUT WAS THAT THE "VAMPIRE" PROBABLY WASN'T CHASING US AT **ALL**.

HE WAS **BEING** CHASED...

...BY MY DOG.

TOGO!

TOGO LIKES TO COME ALONG WHEN I GO OUT SOMETIMES, AND I GUESS I FORGOT TO LATCH HIS DOGGIE-DOOR!

HEY, IF HE *WASN'T* A REAL VAMPIRE, WHY ISN'T HE HERE ON LINE WITH THE REST OF US?

MAYBE HE'S ALREADY *INSIDE?*

ONCE WE WERE WATCHING THE MOVIE, I WAS *AMAZED.* NOT BY THE FILM, BUT BY HOW BESS AND GEORGE COULD SEE SOMETHING SO *MANY* TIMES AND STILL BE TOTALLY *GRIPPED!*

IT'S SO *ROMANTIC!*

AND TERRIFYING!

I KIND OF GOT OVER THE WHOLE VAMPIRE THING AFTER I READ *DRACULA* IN THE FIFTH GRADE.

I DON'T KNOW, THE WHOLE BLOOD-SUCKING THING JUST DIDN'T APPEAL.

CRIMES ASIDE, ONE OF THE BIGGEST MYSTERIES I'VE EVER TRIED TO SOLVE IS WHY PEOPLE LIKE WHAT THEY LIKE.

STILL WORKING ON THAT ONE.

I DID NOTICE THAT THE GUY FROM THE GRAVEYARD *WASN'T* HERE. MAYBE HE WAS GOING TO A *LATER* SHOW?

I ALSO NOTICED SOMETHING ELSE.

MAYBE I WAS JUST SO *BORED* WITH THE MOVIE, I WAS LOOKING FOR SOMETHING TO DISTRACT ME.

BUT THIS WAS A BIG *SOCIAL* THING FOR ALL THE *DIELITE* FANS IN RIVER HEIGHTS.

SO WHY WAS *ONE* GIRL IN THE ENTIRE THEATER SITTING *ALONE?*

I WILL NOT CRY! I PROMISED!

IT'S SO SAD! THEY *CAN'T* BE TOGETHER FOREVER! NOT EVEN A *WEEK!* ⸱SOB!⸱

GUYS... DO YOU KNOW THAT *GIRL* SITTING BACK THERE?

MISS CREEPY IN THE CLOAK...? SHE'S BEEN IN THE SAME SPOT FOR *EVERY* SHOW, MORNING TO NIGHT.

ALL OF THEM? HOW WOULD *YOU* KNOW THAT UNLESS YOU WERE-- ? NEVER MIND.

OKAY, SO IT WASN'T *STRANGE* TO BE *OBSESSED* ABOUT THIS PARTICULAR MOVIE.

BUT THERE WAS *SOMETHING* ABOUT HER. I HAD A *HUNCH* THERE WAS A MYSTERY HERE.

AND MY HUNCHES ARE USUALLY RIGHT.

MY HUNCH GOT EVEN STRONGER WHEN, IN A THEATER FULL OF PEOPLE **RIVETED** ON THE SCREEN...

...SHE NOTICED ME WATCHING HER.

AND GOT UP TO LEAVE...

... IN THE **MIDDLE** OF THE MOVIE.

AND SHE DIDN'T EVEN SEEM **BORED**, LIKE I WAS.

PART OF ME WANTED TO **FOLLOW** HER, BUT I HAD NO REAL REASON, SO I WAITED UNTIL THE END.

WHAT'D YOU THINK, HUH?

SHE DIDN'T SEEM LONELY, BUT THERE WAS SOMETHING **TENSE** ABOUT HER.

NO, NO, NO! I DON'T WANT TO KNOW WHAT YOU THOUGHT OF THE **AUDIENCE**!

I WAS ASKING ABOUT THE MOVIE!

THAT? WELL, ISN'T IT KIND OF **SILLY** TO BELIEVE SOME VAMPIRE CAN SNEAK UP ON YOU AND...

GOOD EVENING. I AM *GREGOR COFFSON.*

WE MET *EARLIER...*

IN THE... *GRAVE-YARD?*

⋛*GASP!*⋛

I'M SO *SORRY!* I DIDN'T MEAN TO *STARTLE* YOU!

THEN YOU MIGHT WANT TO RETHINK THE WHOLE *SNEAKING UP* THING! I *SAW* YOU SKULKING BY THAT DOOR.

I WASN'T *SKULKING!* I WAS WAITING FOR YOU! I WANTED TO APOLOGIZE FOR WHAT HAPPENED EARLIER.

WE *KNEW* THAT.

YEAH, WE JUST REALLY *LIKE* GASPING AND FALLING. IT'S GOOD PRACTICE!

I'VE RECENTLY MOVED INTO THE OLD *BENSEN ESTATE,* AND I DON'T REALLY KNOW ANYONE IN TOWN YET.

AND, YOU'RE *ALLERGIC* TO DOGS?

NO, JUST VERY *FRIGHTENED* BY THEM.

BUT *TOGO'S TINY!*

SMALL DOGS ESPE-CIALLY!

MAY I... WALK YOU THROUGH THE PARK?

GREGOR WAS *PALE* AND CONSTANTLY *MOVING*, AS IF HE HAD SOME SORT OF NERVOUS DISEASE. I INSTINCTIVELY FELT *SORRY* FOR HIM, BUT DIDN'T KNOW *WHY*.

WHY? AFRAID OF THE DARK, TOO?

EASY, GEORGE, I DON'T THINK...

I... I'M NOT VERY *GOOD* WITH PEOPLE. SORRY TO HAVE BOTHERED YOU.

HEY! I WAS KIDDING!

YOU SCARED HIM OFF! AND HE WAS COMPLETELY *CUTE!*

OH, FUDGE. MAYBE I CAN APOLOGIZE BY TAKING HIM TO *DINNER!*

I SAW HIM FIRST!

ACTUALLY, WE *ALL* SAW HIM FIRST WHEN HE JUMPED OUT AT US... TWICE!

SO... YOU LIKE HIM, *TOO?*

ME? NO! I JUST LIKE TO KEEP TRACK OF DETAILS. GIRL DETECTIVE, REMEMBER? BESIDES, I HAVE...

YOU'RE A *DETECTIVE?* THAT'S FASCINATING!

I'D *LOVE* TO TALK TO YOU ABOUT THAT, PERHAPS OVER DINNER? OR A MOVIE? OR DINNER *AND* A MOVIE?

THAT WAS UNEXPECTED. ONE MINUTE HE COULD BARELY SPEAK TO US, THE NEXT HE WAS ASKING ME ON A *DATE!*

THANKS... I'M... *FLATTERED,* BUT I ALREADY HAVE A *NED*... I MEAN... BOYFRIEND.

SO?

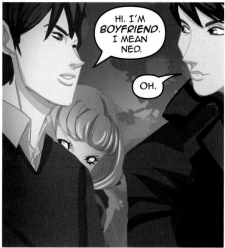

HI. I'M *BOYFRIEND.* I MEAN NED.

OH.

I'M GREGOR, NED. I WOULD LIKE TO TAKE YOUR GIRLFRIEND TO DINNER AND A MOVIE TO TALK ABOUT HER DETECTIVE WORK.

I THINK SHE ALREADY SAID NO.

NED'S *JEALOUS!* THAT'S A *NEW* EMOTION FOR HIM, ISN'T IT?

WELL, THERE HASN'T BEEN MUCH *COMPETITION* HAS THERE? AND A *VAMPIRE* IS TOUGH TO BEAT!

TELL ME ABOUT IT! CHECK OUT THAT PALE SKIN, THOSE *CLOTHES*! WOOF!

HEY! PRIVATE CONVER-SATION, DEE-DEE!

DON'T *CALL* ME THAT!

IN FACT, DON'T CALL ME AT *ALL*!

VAMPIRE BOY MAY NOT BE INTERESTED, BUT *I* SEE AN OPENING TO PUT THE BITE ON MR. NED NICKERSON! HA-HA-HA!

OH, PLEASE! YOU'VE BEEN TRYING TO GET NED FOR AGES!

AND BESIDES, VAMPIRE-GIRLS DON'T LAUGH LIKE THAT! ONLY *WITCHES* DO! WITCH!

GREGOR WAS CERTAINLY *MYSTERIOUS*, BUT MUCH AS I LOVE A GOOD MYSTERY, BY MORNING THE ONLY THING I WAS THINKING ABOUT WAS HOW TO GET BESS AND GEORGE TO LET *ME* PICK THE NEXT MOVIE.

THAT IS UNTIL *HANNAH GRUEN*, OUR HOUSEKEEPER, OPENED THE DOOR.

I *WOULD* HAVE LET YOU SLEEP THE DAY AWAY, NANCY, BUT A DELIVERY MAN CAME WITH SOMETHING FOR *YOU*.

DID YOU AND *NED* FIGHT?

I DON'T *THINK* SO...

POOR NED, SOMETIMES I'M SO BUSY SOLVING CRIMES I CAN'T QUITE REMEMBER WHAT WE SAID TO EACH OTHER LAST.

THESE AREN'T FROM NED! NO ONE WHO **KNOWS** ME WOULD SEND ME THIS!

I MEAN... **A HUNDRED FIVE MINUTE MYSTERIES?** THAT SHOULD TAKE ABOUT A **MINUTE**...

IT WAS FROM **GREGOR.** HE WANTED TO MEET ME FOR COFFEE AT DUSK.

HE SAID IT WAS IMPORTANT, AND THAT IT WASN'T A **DATE**, SO NED SHOULDN'T WORRY, **IF** I TOLD HIM.

OF COURSE I **DID** TELL NED, AND WHEN HE ASKED WHY I WANTED TO GO, I GAVE HIM TWO REASONS.

THE **FIRST** WAS THAT I FELT SORT OF BAD FOR GREGOR, HE WAS NEW IN TOWN AND SEEMED TROUBLED. **SOMEONE** SHOULD BE NICE TO HIM.

THE **SECOND** WAS THAT I FOUND THE WHOLE THING VERY **MYSTERIOUS** AND ABSOLUTELY **HAD** TO FIND OUT WHAT WAS GOING ON.

THAT **SECOND** REASON NED UNDERSTOOD **COMPLETELY**. HE GETS ME.

IS IT OKAY TO PULL THE CHAIR OUT FOR YOU?

AS LONG AS YOU DON'T PULL IT OUT FROM **UNDER** ME!

GREGOR, ON THE OTHER HAND, DIDN'T EVEN GET MY *JOKES*. HE SEEMED SO SELF-CONSCIOUS, WORRIED ABOUT DOING *ANYTHING* I MIGHT CONSIDER WRONG.

I'M SORRY...

ABOUT WHAT?

JUST IN GENERAL! I'M AFRAID I'M NOT VERY USED TO BEING AROUND PEOPLE.

BUT I *KNEW* I HAD TO MAKE SOME EFFORT TO GET TO KNOW YOU. I NEED YOUR *HELP!*

I *WANT* TO TRUST YOU, BUT I DON'T KNOW IF I *CAN!*

I DON'T KNOW IF I CAN TRUST *ANYONE*...

THAT MUST BE VERY HARD. I CAN'T *IMAGINE* NOT HAVING SOMEONE TO TALK TO.

I COULDN'T HELP BUT FEEL FLATTERED THAT HE WANTED TO CONFIDE IN ME.

I REALIZED, THOUGH, THAT LEARNING HIS SECRETS WOULD TAKE *TIME*.

I KNEW THAT MEANT MY PALS WOULD *TALK*.

IS NANCY LIKE *DATING* A VAMPIRE NOW? SHE'S SEEN HIM EVERY DAY FOR A *WEEK!*

EVERY *NIGHT* YOU MEAN! HOPE SHE'S NOT FALLING UNDER HIS *SPELL!*

"THEY'VE BEEN WALKING IN THE PARK, DOING 'RESEARCH' AT THE LIBRARY, DRINKING COFFEE!"

"SHE EVEN INVITED HIM *HOME!* OF COURSE THAT DIDN'T WORK OUT BECAUSE OF HIS FEAR OF DOGS, BUT STILL..."

SO WHAT? NANCY'S NEVER DONE *ANYTHING* TO MAKE ME JEALOUS!

UNTIL *NOW!* DO YOU REALIZE HOW *GREAT* YOUR BROW LOOKS WHEN IT *FURROWS* LIKE THAT?

THERE WERE *REASONS* DEIRDRE AND I DIDN'T GET ALONG.

BUT I COULD ALWAYS COUNT ON MY *FRIENDS* NOT TO JUMP TO THE WRONG CONCLUSIONS!

NOTHING?

NOT EVEN A MYFACEPLACE PAGE! GREGOR COFFSON IS A *TOTAL* BLANK!

ALL I KNOW IS THAT HE'S NEVER LIVED IN THE SAME TOWN FOR MORE THAN A *YEAR!*

WHY WOULD SOMEONE KEEP MOVING LIKE THAT?

UNLESS...

HE'S A REAL VAMPIRE!

WELL, I COULD COUNT ON THEM NOT TO JUMP TO THE WRONG CONCLUSIONS ABOUT *ME* ANYWAY.

FINALLY, THOUGH, I FELT LIKE I WAS GETTING SOME- WHERE WITH THE MYSTERIOUS GREGOR COFFSON.

IT'S BEEN SO *HARD* TO GAIN HIS TRUST, BUT HE'S INVITED ME TO DINNER TO DISCUSS SOMETHING "IMPORTANT."

SOMETHING... "IMPORTANT"?

OVER "DINNER"?

I'M SURE HE'S GOING TO TALK ABOUT HIS *SECRET!*

UM... NANCY...

SUPPOSE IT'S A *DANGEROUS* SECRET?

LIKE MAYBE HE *FEEDS* OFF OF PEOPLE?

YOU GUYS DON'T REALLY *BELIEVE* THAT VAMPIRE STUFF, DO YOU?

WELL, I THINK IT'S *FINE* HE TRUSTS YOU SO MUCH! JUST GREAT! *TOTALLY* GREAT!

IN FACT, IT'S THE *GREATEST* THING I'VE *EVER* HEARD!

IT'S SO TOTALLY *FANTASTIC* I THINK I'LL TAKE A NICE LONG *WALK* AND JUST *THINK* ABOUT HOW *GREAT* IT IS!

NED?

HE SEEMS SO *UPSET*, BUT IT'S GETTING *LATE!* I HAVE TO GET READY FOR THE *DINNER!*

HE'LL BE *FINE*, RIGHT? HE *UNDER-STANDS!*

WOW, NANCY IS IGNORING NED JUST TO SOLVE A MYSTERY!

YOU KNOW WHAT *THIS* MEANS, RIGHT?

OH, YEAH.

VAMPIRES ARE REAL!

AND NANCY IS FALLING UNDER HIS *SPELL!*

I'M *GOOD* WITH CRIME, BUT SOMETIMES I CAN BE TOTALLY *DENSE* ABOUT THINGS LIKE KEEPING MY GAS TANK FULL OR BEING AWARE OF MY BOYFRIEND'S FEELINGS.

GREAT.

PERFECT.

TERRIFIC.

OR HOW *LOW* DEIRDRE WILL SINK!

IT'S *ALWAYS* TERRIFIC WHEN I RUN INTO *YOU*, NED!

DON'T LOOK SO GLUM! TAKE A LADY FOR A WALK!

≳GRUMBLE≲ ≳GRUMBLE≲

ISN'T THIS NICER THAN *MOPING* OVER SOME SILLY GIRL DETECTIVE?

OH, LOOK! ISN'T THAT THE RESTAURANT WHERE NANCY'S HAVING DINNER WITH GREGOR?

IT *IS*! WHAT A COINCI-DENCE!

AND DON'T *THEY* LOOK SNUG!

THAT'S IT! I HAVE HAD *ENOUGH!* I'M GONNA... I'M GONNA...

HEAD *HOME* AND READ A *BOOK* OR SOMETHING...

SEE YOU SOON, I HOPE!

I DO SO *ENJOY* OUR TIME TOGETHER, NED DEAR!

GREGOR, I'M *GLAD* YOU'RE BEGINNING TO TRUST ME, BUT YOU DO KNOW THAT *NED* IS MY BOYFRIEND, RIGHT?

OF *COURSE!*

I'D NEVER DREAM OF TRYING TO COME BETWEEN THE TWO OF YOU. IT'S JUST THAT IT'S BEEN SO... *LONELY!*

IF VAMPIRES *AREN'T* REAL, WHY ARE THERE SO MANY BOOKS ABOUT THEM?

HUH... I'VE FOUND SOME *POLICE* FILES WITH GREGOR'S NAME ON THEM, BUT THEY'RE *SEALED*. PROBABLY JUST *PARKING TICKETS*...

OH, MAYBE NANCY'S RIGHT, AND WE'RE SILLY TO WORRY ABOUT SOME CREATURE OF THE NIGHT THAT CAN COME *SWOOPING* OUT OF NOWHERE AND...

÷GRUMBLE÷ ÷GRUMBLE÷ ÷GRUMBLE÷

YIKES!

NED!

JUST THE GUY WE WANT TO SEE!

LOOK, IT'S NOT *DEFINITE*, BUT WE THINK THERE MAY BE SOMETHING *FISHY* ABOUT GREGG COFFSON!

GREAT!

I MEAN... OH, NO! IS NANCY IN SOME KIND OF *DANGER!* LET'S GO STOP THAT DINNER *IMMEDIATELY!*

YEAH, WELL WE DON'T HAVE ANY *PROOF.*

AND YOU *KNOW* HOW NANCY GETS ABOUT THE WHOLE *PROOF* THING...

"SO WE WERE THINKING YOU COULD HELP US BREAK INTO HIS HOUSE AND *INVESTIGATE* IT!"

WHAT AM I EXPECTING TO *FIND*, ANYWAY?

IT'S NOT LIKE A *REAL* VAMPIRE WOULD LEAVE HIS COFFIN JUST LYING AROUND.

WOULD HE?

OKAY, SO MAYBE I *SHOULDN'T* FEEL SO *BAD* ABOUT SNEAKING IN HERE!

LITTLE DID MY DEAR *TRUSTING* PALS REALIZE THAT THEY'D FORGOTTEN THE FIRST RULE OF DETECTIVE WORK – THE SUSPECT ALWAYS RETURNS TO THE HOUSE *WHILE* YOU'RE SEARCHING IT!

THANKS SO MUCH FOR THE DINNER, GREGOR, BUT YOU *STILL* HAVEN'T TOLD ME WHAT THE BIG SECRET IS!

I *WILL*... BUT COULD WE PLEASE GO INSIDE FIRST?

EEP! INCOMING!

NED! THEY'RE BACK!

I KNOW! WHAT SHOULD WE DO?

COME ON, GUYS! DON'T YOU REMEMBER ANYTHING NANCY TAUGHT US?

HIDE!

CLOSE THE WINDOW, SO THE WIND DOESN'T MOVE THE DRAPES AND HE'LL *NEVER* SPOT US!

WHAT IF HE HAS *X-RAY-VISION?*

THAT'S *SUPERMAN,* BESS! WE *SHOULD* REALLY BE WORRIED ABOUT WHETHER OR NOT *NANCY'S* ABOUT TO BECOME HIS *VICTIM!*

WOW! THAT IS *GREAT* VEGETABLE JUICE!

I WAS *BOUND* TO GET GOOD AT MAKING IT.

IT'S PRACTICALLY *ALL* I EAT.

I HAVE A RARE DISEASE, *ERYTHROPOIETIC PORPHYRIA.*

ISN'T THERE A THEORY THAT LONG AGO PORPHYRIA LED TO STORIES ABOUT *VAMPIRES?*

THAT'S NOT *ENTIRELY* TRUE.

THERE ARE EIGHT KINDS OF PORPHYRIA, BUT ONLY *FOUR* LEAVE THEIR SUFFERERS PALE AND UNABLE TO STAND SUNLIGHT.

IF UNTREATED, IT CAN ALSO LEAD TO BOUTS OF MENTAL ILLNESS. KING GEORGE III FROM ENGLAND IS BELIEVED TO HAVE SUFFERED FROM IT.

IT *IS* ONE OF THE TYPES I HAVE.

I REQUIRE REGULAR BLOOD TRANSFUSIONS, AND I HAVE TO REMAIN IN THE DARK AT ALL TIMES.

IT'S NOT AN *EASY* LIFE.

GREGOR, I'M SO SORRY.

AND *HOW* IS IT YOU EXPLAIN THE COFFIN IN YOUR PARLOR?

THAT? IT'S JUST SOMETHING THE *LAST TENANT* LEFT.

OF COURSE! DAN THE MAGICIAN! I HELPED HIM FIND HIS MISSING ASSISTANT.*

THIS PLACE IS *FULL* OF THE WEIRD STUFF HE USED FOR HIS MAGIC SHOW.

I'M *SORRY* IT'S TAKEN SO LONG FOR ME TO TELL YOU, NANCY. I DIDN'T KNOW... WHETHER YOU... WHETHER YOU REALLY *LIKED* ME OR NOT.

*SEE NANCY DREW GRAPHIC NOVEL #14 "SLEIGHT OF DAN."

THAT WAS A SURPRISE.

SUDDENLY, HANDSOME, MYSTERIOUS GREGOR SOUNDED LESS LIKE A VAMPIRE AND MORE LIKE A TEN YEAR OLD.

THAT'S WHEN IT DAWNED ON ME. GREGOR *WASN'T* ALOOF.

HE WAS JUST TERRIBLY *AWKWARD* AROUND PEOPLE BECAUSE HIS DISEASE HAS MADE HIM LEAD SUCH AN ISOLATED LIFE.

WHICH MEANT I HAD TO BE VERY *CAREFUL* WITH HIM.

SIT WITH ME.

WAIT A MINUTE...

I DIDN'T WANT TO REJECT HIM, BUT I DIDN'T WANT HIM TO GET THE WRONG IDEA, EITHER.

PLEASE?

HE'D BEEN ALONE AND LONELY SO LONG, HE MIGHT FALL *IN LOVE* WITH ANY GIRL WHO *SMILED* AT HIM.

OKAY, BUT WE'RE JUST *FRIENDS*, RIGHT?

NED IS MY BOY-FRIEND.

I UNDER-STAND.

BUT NANCY, MY CONDITION *ISN'T* MY BIG SECRET. I HAVE A MUCH MORE *SERIOUS* PROBLEM.

SOME HORRIBLE PERSON HAS BEEN *STALKING* ME. THEY'RE *CONVINCED* I'M REALLY A VAMPIRE!

"THEY'VE SENT THREATENING NOTES, WARNING OF THEIR PLANS TO *DESTROY* ME!"

"BAD ENOUGH WHEN THE NOTES ARE TEXTED, OR SENT THROUGH EMAIL, BUT WHEN THEY ARRIVED BY *LETTER* THAT MEANT THE STALKER KNEW WHERE I *LIVED!*"

"THE LETTERS HAVE FOLLOWED ME TO *THREE TOWNS* SO FAR, ALL OVER THE COUNTRY."

"EACH TIME, THE POLICE COULDN'T IDENTIFY THE WRITER, AND I BECAME SO *FRIGHTENED* I WAS FORCED TO *MOVE.*"

NOW I'M GETTING *TEXTED* HERE IN RIVER HEIGHTS!

HERE, READ THEM.

"*FOUND YOU AGAIN, FOUL CREATURE! THIS TIME YOU WILL NOT ESCAPE ME!*"

ONCE THEY TEXT, SOMEHOW, THEY'RE ABLE TO FIND OUT WHERE I LIVE. IT'S ONLY A MATTER OF TIME.

BUT I DON'T WANT TO *RUN* ANYMORE. I'M *SICK* OF IT!

SO I'VE TAKEN *MEASURES* TO PROTECT MYSELF.

MEASURES? WHAT DO YOU MEAN?

IT COST A *FORTUNE*, BUT MY FAMILY HAS ALWAYS BEEN *WEALTHY*.

THROUGHOUT THE HOUSE, I'VE SET UP AN ELABORATE SYSTEM OF *ALARMS*...

...AND *TRAPS!*

MANY ARE BASED ON THE *PROPS* THAT MAGICIAN LEFT BEHIND.

WE CAN'T HEAR A *THING*. AND FRANKLY, IT'S NONE OF OUR BUSINESS ANYWAY.

I TRUST NANCY. I'M GOING HOME.

PERFECT! THE WINDOW IS *STUCK* NOW!

THE KITCHEN HAD A DOOR TO THE BASEMENT. MAYBE I CAN GET OUT THAT WAY.

WAIT!

THE VAMPIRE WILL *SEE* YOU!

THERE *IS* NO VAMPIRE! IT'S *SILLY*. ALL THAT STUFF WE FOUND MUST HAVE *SOME* EXPLANATION.

OH... MAYBE HE'S *RIGHT*.

RIGHT?

I THINK *WE* SHOULD GO, TOO!

GO?

THEN WHAT'D I BRING *THESE* FOR?

ISN'T THIS IS A LITTLE *EXTREME*?

NO! I'M THROUGH LIVING IN FEAR!

⸮SIGH.⸮

THE ONLY *BRIGHT* SIDE IS IF NO ONE *SEES* ME, I WON'T HAVE TO EXPLAIN MYSELF TO NANCY!

"APPARENTLY THIS MAGICIAN WORKED WITH *TIGERS*."

WHA--?

"AND HE LEFT BEHIND A BIG *CAGE!*"

OH.... NUTS!

NED?

"HE ALSO LEFT BEHIND A *LOT* OF ROPES."

YOU DOWN HERE?

"AND A BOOK ON HOW TO *USE* THEM."

YIKES!

⸘URK?⸘

IT'S UP TO *ME* TO SAVE NANCY *NOW!*

I'LL SCREAM, SCARE HIM WITH THE HAMMER AND STAKE...

...THEN *RUN* LIKE CRAZY!

THE *HARDEST* THING TO INSTALL WAS THE TRAP DOOR.

BUT IT'S MY *FAVORITE!*

OOF! OOF! UNGH! WAY TO STICK TO THE PLAN -- I EVEN *FORGOT* TO SCREAM!

I *STILL* DON'T FEEL COMPLETELY SAFE, NANCY!

IF THERE'S *ANYTHING* YOU CAN DO TO FIND THIS PERSON AND MAKE THEM STOP, I'D BE GRATEFUL *FOREVER*!

FOREVER'S A *LONG* TIME, BUT I *AM* A DETECTIVE, SO....

BREEP! BREEP! BREEP!

WELL, *THAT* DOESN'T SOUND GOOD!

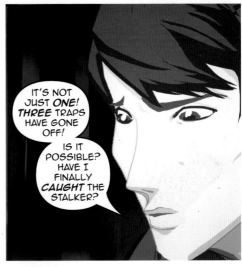

IT'S NOT JUST *ONE*! *THREE* TRAPS HAVE GONE OFF!

IS IT POSSIBLE? HAVE I FINALLY *CAUGHT* THE STALKER?

IF HE *HAD*, THIS MIGHT JUST BE THE *SHORTEST* CASE I'D EVER WORKED ON!

BUT IT *WASN'T* THE STALKER.

NOT *GREGOR'S* STALKER, ANYWAY!

IT WAS MY THREE CLOSEST FRIENDS, WITH A *LOT* OF EXPLAINING TO DO.

NANCY! GREGOR! WHATEVER ARE *YOU* TWO DOING HERE? HI!

I KNOW THIS LOOKS KIND OF BAD, BUT WE CAN *EXPLAIN!*

NO, WE *CAN'T*, NOT *REALLY.*

GEORGE THOUGHT GREGOR WAS A VAMPIRE, AND *SHE'S* THE SMART ONE!

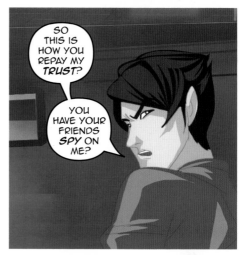

SO THIS IS HOW YOU REPAY MY *TRUST?*

YOU HAVE YOUR FRIENDS *SPY* ON ME?

YOU'RE TRYING TO *DESTROY* ME JUST LIKE THE STALKER!

GREGOR, I HAD *NO* IDEA THEY WERE HERE!

AND YOU, HOW *DARE* YOU BREAK IN HERE!

GEE, NANCE, COME ON! *YOU* BREAK INTO HOUSES ALL THE TIME!

YEAH, BUT THAT'S WHEN I THINK SOMEONE'S A *CROOK*, NOT A *VAMPIRE!*

I KNOW IT WAS VERY HARD FOR YOU TO TRUST ME AT ALL, PLEASE DON'T LET THIS TURN YOU AWAY!

I *PROMISE* NOTHING LIKE THIS WILL HAPPEN AGAIN.

LET ME PROVE IT. LET ME BE YOUR FRIEND AND *HELP* YOU!

WELL...

OKAY.

HEY, WOULD YOU MIND, YOU KNOW, NOT *TOUCHING* HIM ON THE SHOULDER LIKE THAT?

FOR HEAVEN'S SAKE, YOU'RE NOT *JEALOUS*... ARE YOU?

ME? NO... I... UHM...

IT'S JUST THAT... WELL, I... OH...

HEY, WAIT A MINUTE. ARE YOU *ENJOYING* THIS?

NO! NANCY AND I ARE JUST FRIENDS... RIGHT, NANCY?

RIGHT.

BUT IF YOU REALLY WANT ME TO TRUST YOU, LIKE YOU SAY...

...THEN YOU'LL TELL YOUR FRIENDS TO LEAVE *NOW!*

HEY!

WE *ARE* SORRY!

AND ANY FRIEND OF NANCY *HAS* TO BE A FRIEND OF *OURS*, RIGHT?

THIS WAS A TOUGH ONE. THESE GUYS HAD ALWAYS BEEN MY CLOSEST PALS. WE'D BEEN THROUGH *EVERYTHING* TOGETHER.

BUT CLEARLY *THEY* DIDN'T TRUST ME, AND GREGOR WAS VERY SKITTISH TO BEGIN WITH, SO...

NO. I'M SORRY, BUT YOU'VE GOT TO *LEAVE* GREGOR'S HOUSE.

NOW.

SORRY WE THOUGHT YOU WERE A VAMPIRE, GREGOR.

YEAH, WHAT *SHE* SAID.

BUT I *DID* SEE THAT LOOK ON HIS FACE.

BE CARE-FUL.

GLICK

REALLY BLEW THAT, HUH?

IT *COULD* HAVE GONE BETTER.

BUT DON'T YOU THINK THAT ALARM SYSTEM IS KIND OF *FREAKY?*

YEAH. WHAT IS HE *AFRAID* OF?

MAYBE I COULD DO MORE COMPUTER RESEARCH ON HIM?

IF YOU DO, COUNT ME *OUT!*

I'D LIKE NANCY TO SPEAK TO ME AGAIN *SOMETIME* THIS YEAR.

"I WILL SAY *ONE* THING ABOUT THAT ALARM SYSTEM, THOUGH."

"GREGOR WILL *NEVER* HAVE TO WORRY ABOUT A *THIEF!*"

SNIP!

RURRURURURMRMMMMBLLLLLEEE

WATCH OUT FOR PAPERCUT

Welcome to the premiere edition of the all-new NANCY DREW graphic novel series! I'm Jim Salicrup, Editor-in-Chief of Papercutz, publisher of graphic novels for all-ages. If you were a follower of Nancy's first graphic novel series, welcome back! If you're new to Nancy Drew in comics form, well, you're in for a real treat! Nancy Drew is just as fun and exciting in comics form as she is in her prose series.

In fact, we strive to preserve all the wonderful things that have made Nancy Drew so popular and successful in her book series in our all-new graphic novel stories. Artist Sho Murase and Carlos Guzman do an amazing job of bringing Nancy, Bess, George, Ned, and the rest to comics life. Many people have said that our NANCY DREW graphic novels are like seeing an animated movie on paper! Writers Stefan Petrucha and Sarah Kinney are always finding challenging new mysteries for the world famous Girl Detective, and considering that 2010 is the 80th anniversary of Nancy Drew that is no easy task! Nancy has virtually done it all! But she's never met a vampire before… or has she?

Years ago, Nancy, along with The Hardy Boys, shared a prime time network TV series on ABC. If you track down a DVD of the second season opener of "The Hardy Boys/Nancy Drew Mysteries" series from September 11 and 18 1977 you'll find the two-part episode "The Hardy Boys and Nancy Drew Meet Dracula"! Was he really Dracula? Who knows?

And what about Nancy Drew becoming a "vampire slayer"..? Crazy idea? Well, we know of one vampire who may not think so-- in season 4, episode 21 of "Buffy the Vampire Slayer," Spike, a vampire, looks at Buffy and says "Look at little Nancy Drew."

If you're one of those people new to the NANCY DREW graphic novels, and you're looking to find more NANCY DREW graphic novels to enjoy, let me direct your attention to page two. You'll find lots of wonderful NANCY DREW graphic novels to choose from. They're available at booksellers everywhere, but if your favorite bookseller is out of stock, you can always order directly from us—but we suggest trying bookstores and online booksellers first. And if you're already a fan of NANCY DREW graphic novels, you can order any of the books you're missing! Who doesn't want a complete collection of NANCY DREW graphic novels after all?

And as much as we love Nancy Drew, we at Papercutz actually publish other graphic novels you might enjoy as well! There's THE HARDY BOYS, of course! And Tinker Bell stars in the DISNEY FAIRIES graphic novels. If sci-fi action appeals to you, we suggest BIONICLE graphic novels based on the LEGO constructible action figures. For fun-filled adventure, you can't beat the GERONIMO STILTON graphic novels. But in the spirit of NANCY DREW "Vampire Hunter," we suggest you check out "The Scarlet Letter," a comics adaptation of the Nathaniel Hawthorne novel by P. Craig Russell and Jill Thompson. While the Scarlet Letter is a far more serious story than "Vampire Hunter," both stories feature a character that is misjudged by others. On the following pages, we're presenting an excerpt from the CLASSICS ILLUSTRATED Graphic Novel #6 "The Scarlet Letter." We hope you enjoy it. For information on other CLASSICS ILLUSTRATED titles, and everything else Papercutz is up to, visit www. papercutz.com.

Let us know what you think of this graphic novel—write to us at Nancy Drew c/o PAPERCUTZ, 40 Exchange Place, Suite 1308, New York, NY 10005 or send an email to me at salicrup@papercutz.com. We love hearing what you think, and appreciate any thoughts, comments, and even criticisms you may have. Don't be shy—write to Papercutz and let your voice be heard!

Until we meet again, keep sleuthing!

Thanks,

PRESENTING AN ALL-NEW SERIES FROM PAPERCUTZ...

COMING FALL 2010!

A LANE WAS OPENED THROUGH THE CROWD. HESTER PRYNNE SET FORTH TOWARDS THE PLACE APPOINTED FOR HER PUNISHMENT...

THIS SCAFFOLD WAS HELD TO BE AS EFFECTUAL AN AGENT IN THE PROMOTION OF GOOD CITIZENSHIP AS WAS THE GUILLOTINE AMONG THE TERRORISTS OF FRANCE.

...AND CAME AT LENGTH TO A SORT OF SCAFFOLD.

HESTER'S SENTENCE BORE THAT SHE SHOULD STAND A CERTAIN TIME UPON THE PLATFORM.

KNOWING HER PART, SHE ASCENDED A FLIGHT OF STEPS...

...AND WAS DISPLAYED TO THE MULTITUDE.

THE UNHAPPY CULPRIT SUSTAINED HERSELF AS BEST A WOMAN MIGHT, UNDER THE WEIGHT OF A THOUSAND UNRELENTING EYES, ALL FASTENED UPON HER AND CONCENTRATED AT HER BOSOM.

IT WAS ALMOST INTOLERABLE TO BE BORNE.

YET THERE WERE INTERVALS WHEN THE WHOLE SCENE SEEMED TO GLIMMER INDISTINCTLY, LIKE A MASS OF IMPERFECTLY SHAPED AND SPECTRAL IMAGES. REMINISCENCES CAME SWARMING BACK; ONE PICTURE PRECISELY AS VIVID AS ANOTHER.

SHE SAW AGAIN HER NATIVE VILLAGE, IN OLD ENGLAND, AND HER PATERNAL HOME.

SHE SAW HER FATHER'S FACE, WITH ITS BALD BROW AND WHITE BEARD, AND HER MOTHER'S FACE, WITH ITS LOOK OF HEEDFUL AND ANXIOUS LOVE.

SHE SAW A MAN WELL STRICKEN IN YEARS, WITH EYES DIM AND BLEARED, WHOSE FIGURE WAS SLIGHTLY DEFORMED.

SHE SAW A CITY, WHERE A NEW LIFE HAD AWAITED HER.

LASTLY, CAME THE RUDE MARKETPLACE, WITH ALL THE PURITAN TOWNSPEOPLE LEVELLING THEIR STERN REGARDS AT HESTER PRYNNE--WHO STOOD ON THE SCAFFOLD, AN INFANT IN HER ARM, AND THE LETTER "A" IN SCARLET, UPON HER BOSOM.

I PRAY YOU, WHO IS THIS WOMAN -- AND WHERE-FORE IS SHE SET UP TO PUBLIC SHAME?

YOU MUST BE A STRANGER IN THIS REGION, ELSE YOU WOULD HAVE HEARD... SHE HATH RAISED A GREAT SCANDAL IN GODLY MASTER DIMMESDALE'S CHURCH.

TRUE, I AM A STRANGER, AND HAVE BEEN A WANDERER. I HAVE MET WITH MIS-HAPS BY SEA AND LAND. WHAT HAS BROUGHT THIS WOMAN TO YONDER SCAFFOLD?

SHE WAS THE WIFE OF A LEARNED MAN, ENGLISH BY BIRTH, WHO WAS MINDED TO CROSS OVER AND CAST HIS LOT WITH US.

HE SENT HIS WIFE BEFORE HIM, BUT... BEING LEFT TO HER OWN AFFAIRS...

AND WHO MAY BE THE FATHER OF YONDER BABE?

OF THAT MATTER, MADAM HESTER REFUSETH TO SPEAK, BUT SINCE, MOST LIKELY, HER HUSBAND IS AT THE BOTTOM OF THE SEA, THE EXTREMITY OF OUR LAW -- DEATH -- HAS NOT BEEN PUT IN FORCE.

MERCIFULLY, SHE HAS BEEN DOOMED TO STAND ONLY THREE HOURS ON THE PLATFORM, AND THEN, FOR THE REMAINDER OF HER LIFE, TO WEAR A MARK OF SHAME UPON HER BOSOM.

A WISE SENTENCE! BUT IT IRKS ME THAT HER PARTNER SHOULD NOT STAND ON THE SCAFFOLD BY HER SIDE. BUT HE WILL BE KNOWN! -- HE WILL BE KNOWN!

HEARKEN UNTO ME, HESTER PRYNNE.

I HAVE STRIVEN WITH MY YOUNG BROTHER HERE, UNDER WHOSE PREACHING YOU HAVE SAT, THAT HE SHOULD DEAL WITH YOU, IN HEARING OF ALL -- THAT YOU SHOULD REVEAL THE NAME OF HIM WHO TEMPTED YOU TO THIS VILE, GRIEVOUS FALL.

BUT HE OPPOSES ME THAT IT WERE WRONGING THE VERY NATURE OF WOMAN TO FORCE HER TO LAY OPEN HER HEART'S SECRETS IN SUCH BROAD DAYLIGHT.

WHAT SAY YOU TO IT, ONCE AGAIN, BROTHER DIMMESDALE? IT IS OF MOMENT TO HER SOUL, AND, THEREFORE, MOMENTOUS TO THINE OWN, IN WHOSE CHARGE HERS IS.

EXHORT HER TO CONFESS THE TRUTH!

HESTER PRYNNE, THOU HEAREST WHAT THIS GOOD MAN SAYS, AND SEEST THE ACCOUNTABILITY UNDER WHICH I LABOR.

BE NOT SILENT FROM ANY PITY AND TENDERNESS FOR THE CULPRIT.

BELIEVE ME, HESTER, THOUGH HE WERE TO STEP DOWN FROM A HIGH PLACE, AND STAND THERE BESIDE THEE ON THY PEDESTAL OF SHAME...

...BETTER WERE IT SO THAN TO HIDE A GUILTY HEART THROUGH LIFE.

SPEAK OUT THE NAME OF THY FELLOW-SINNER AND FELLOW-SUFFERER!

Get the complete story in CLASSICS ILLUSTRATED Graphic Novel
#6 "The Scarlet Letter"! Available at booksellers everywhere!